What Bunny Loves

By Cyndy Szekeres

A Golden Book • New York

Western Publishing Company, Inc., Racine, Wisconsin 53404

MCMXCII

This is Bunny.

This is what Bunny loves.

Bunny loves Mother.

Bunny loves Daddy.

Bunny loves the little one.

Bunny has fun with him.

Bunny loves to run.

He runs around a tree.

Bunny loves to make cake.

He loves to eat cake!

Bunny loves to play.

He plays with his friend.

He plays with a little car.

He plays with a big ball.

16

Bunny loves to put on hats—
big hats and little hats.

He loves to ride.

Bunny loves to work.

He loves to make things.

22

Bunny loves all
good things to eat.

Bunny loves to help Daddy.

Bunny loves to read.

Bunny loves to paint.

Bunny loves his boat.

Bunny loves a ride on Daddy…

...all the way to bed!

Good night, Bunny!